The Greatest Creatures on Earth

U0061817

商務印書館（香港）有限公司
http://www.commercialpress.com.hk

CENGAGE
Learning™

Australia • Brazil • Japan • Korea • Mexico • Singapore • Spain • United Kingdom • United States

Director of Content Development:
Anita Raducanu
Series Editor: Rob Waring
Editorial Manager: Bryan Fletcher

Associate Development Editors:
Victoria Forrester, Catherine McCue
責任編輯：黃家麗

出版：

商務印書館（香港）有限公司
香港筲箕灣耀興道3號東匯廣場8樓

Cengage Learning
Units 808-810, 8th floor,
Tins Enterprises Centre,
777 Lai Chi Kok Road, Cheung Sha Wan,
Kowloon, Hong Kong

網址：http://www.commercialpress.com.hk

http://www.cengageasia.com

發行：香港聯合書刊物流有限公司
　　　香港新界大埔汀麗路36號中華商務
　　　印刷大廈3字樓

印刷：中華商務彩色印刷有限公司
版次：2010年3月第1版第2次印刷

ISBN: 978-962-07-1866-3

出版說明

本館一向倡導優質閱讀，近年連續推出以"Q"為標誌的優質英語學習系列(*Quality English Learning*)，其中《Black Cat 優質英語階梯閱讀》，讀者反應令人鼓舞，先後共推出超過60本。

為進一步推動閱讀，本館引入Cengage 出版之*Footprint Library*，使用*National Geographic*的圖像及語料，編成百科英語階梯閱讀系列，有別於Black Cat 古典文學閱讀，透過現代真實題材，百科英語語境能幫助讀者認識今日的世界各事各物，擴闊視野，提高認識及表達英語的能力。

本系列屬non-fiction (非虛構故事類)讀本，結合閱讀、視像和聽力三種學習功能，是一套三合一多媒介讀本，每本書的英文文章以headwords寫成，headwords 選收自以下數據庫的語料：*Collins Cobuild The Bank of English*、*British National Corpus* 及 *BYU Corpus of American English* 等，並配上精彩照片，另加一張video/audio 兩用DVD。編排由淺入深，按級提升，只要讀者堅持學習，必能有效提高英語溝通能力。

商務印書館(香港)有限公司

編輯部

使用説明

百科英語階梯閱讀分四級，共八本書，是彩色有影有聲書，每本有英語文章供閱讀，根據數據庫如 *Collins Cobuild The Bank of English*、*British National Corpus* 及 *BYU Corpus of American English* 選收常用字詞編寫，配彩色照片及一張video/audio 兩用DVD，結合閱讀、聆聽、視像三種學習方式。

讀者可使用本書：

 學習新詞彙，並透過延伸閱讀(Expansion Reading) 練習速讀技巧

 聆聽錄音提高聽力，模仿標準英語讀音

 看短片做練習，以提升綜合理解能力

Grammar Focus解釋語法重點，後附練習題，供讀者即時複習所學，書內其他練習題，有助讀者掌握學習技巧如 scanning, prediction, summarising, identifying the main idea

中英對照生詞表設於書後，既不影響讀者閱讀正文，又具備參考作用

Contents 目錄

出版說明
使用說明

The CD-ROM contains a video and full recording of the text
CD-ROM 包括短片和錄音

Words to Know

This story is set in the
Arctic Ocean.

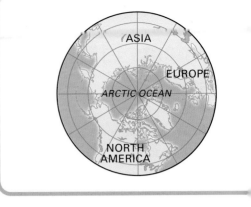

(A) **The Arctic Shore.** Write each word in the picture next to the correct definition.

1. the land next to the ocean: _____.

2. a large white sea animal: _____.

3. hard pieces of water formed in the cold: _____.

4. big stones that you find sometimes find near the sea: _____.

5. a part of the sea that is nearly closed in by land: _____.

6. a large sea animal that has a long object on its head: _____.

shore

narwhal

ice

bay

beluga whale

rocks

The Arctic Shore

B **Arctic Animals.** Look at the pictures and captions. Complete the paragraph below with the correct form of the words in **bold**.

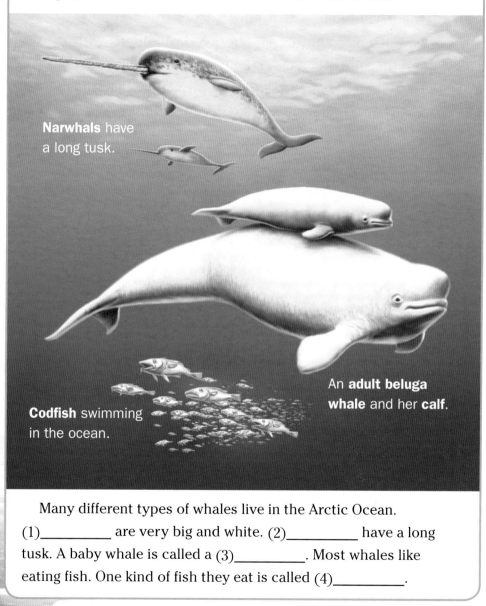

Narwhals have a long tusk.

Codfish swimming in the ocean.

An **adult beluga whale** and her **calf**.

Many different types of whales live in the Arctic Ocean. (1)_____ are very big and white. (2)_____ have a long tusk. A baby whale is called a (3)_____. Most whales like eating fish. One kind of fish they eat is called (4)_____.

Beluga whales are very social animals. This means that they like to be around other whales. Their relationships with the whales around them are very strong. A mother and her calf will often swim together for three years. Beluga whale calves are grey when they are born. They turn white, like the ice around them, when they become adults.

It may seem like the beluga whales have a very happy life, but sometimes this isn't the case …

5

On one particular day, a group of beluga whales is swimming in the bay. When the tide goes out, the adult belugas are able to swim back to deeper water.

However, one young beluga has gone too far onto the shore. It can't get back to the water. Suddenly, play time becomes a **race against time**![1]

---

[1] **race against time:** need to hurry or act quickly

The sun now becomes the whale's biggest danger. It's very hot on the young beluga's body. The whale could easily get sunburn, get too hot, and die. The young beluga has nothing to cover it. It's totally helpless. The other belugas can only watch and wait as the **calf**[1] tries to move.

As the beluga calf **moves around**[2] on the shore, the rocks cut its skin. More and more time passes. The minutes slowly turn into hours. There's nothing that the whale can do for now. It can only wait for the tide to come back.

Everyone has made a mistake in their life. However, this mistake could be deadly for the little beluga. Finally, the tide starts coming back. But will it be soon enough to help the baby beluga?

---

[1]**calf:** a young animal, such as a whale or cow
[2]**move around:** go from one place to another

Predict

Answer the questions. Then scan page 11 to check your answers.

1. What will happen to the beluga calf?

2. Why do you think that?

Slowly the sea starts to come back onto the shore. The water **brings** the very tired beluga **back to life**.[1] It begins to move. Then, it begins to push … and push … and push. With one last energetic push, the beluga is free! At last, it's able to return to the sea.

The young beluga quickly joins the other whales in the deep water once again. The young calf is fine. Perhaps it has learned something from this bad experience. Perhaps it will be more careful next time it's near the shore!

---

[1]**bring … back to life:** give life to sb/sth that is dying

Young belugas are not the only arctic whales that can get into trouble. The narwhal is another type of whale that lives in the Arctic Ocean. They are a very unusual kind of whale. They have a tusk, or horn, that can grow as long as nine feet! The tusk is actually a kind of tooth that grows through the narwhal's top lip. Before, no one knew why the narwhals had this tusk. Most people thought that the whales only used it to fight other whales. However, scientists now think that the tusk helps narwhals sense **environmental conditions**,[1] like temperature.

[1]**environmental conditions:** the state of the natural world

Narwhals usually swim in small groups. However, on this day the number of narwhals swimming together is much larger. The exact number may **vary**,[1] but sometimes the group might grow to more than a hundred whales! The whales are swimming together as they look for one of their favourite foods – codfish.

After a while, the narwhals follow a group of codfish into the bay. But they're taking a big risk. The bay has ice all around it. If the ice moves and closes the opening to the bay, the whales could become **trapped**.[2]

---

[1]**vary:** change
[2]**trapped:** unable to move

And that's exactly what happens! Suddenly, the ice moves in and **closes off**[1] the way out to the open sea. The narwhals can't get out of the bay. They're trapped! Not even their long tusks can help them now …

All the narwhals now have to swim in a very small area of water that has no ice on it. It's a very difficult situation for the narwhals. Whales breathe oxygen. If the ice moves closer and covers the water, the narwhals won't be able to come out of the water. They won't be able to get air! They'll have to swim out from under the ice to find it or they'll die. Will the whales be able to find air **in time**?[2]

---

[1] **close off:** prevent sb from entering a place
[2] **in time:** early enough

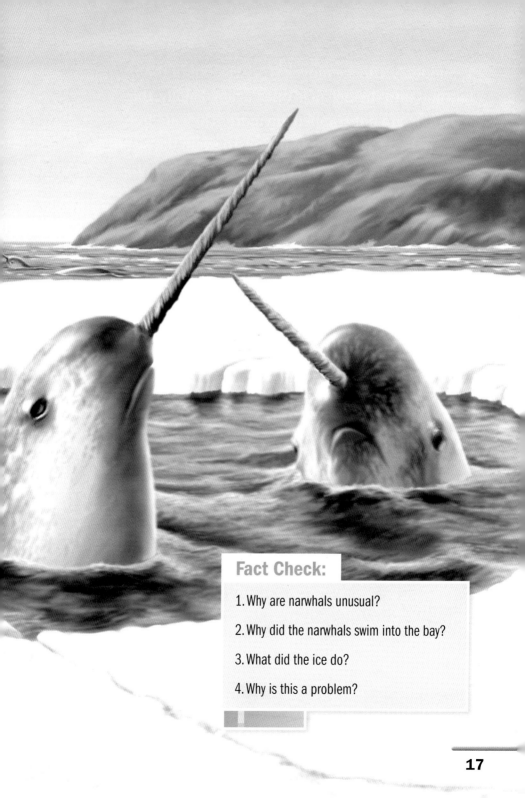

Fact Check:

1. Why are narwhals unusual?

2. Why did the narwhals swim into the bay?

3. What did the ice do?

4. Why is this a problem?

Suddenly, the ice moves. The way out of the
bay and into the ocean is open again. Finally, the
narwhals are not trapped anymore. They are free.
They're free to look for fish. Free to swim the seas.
Free to do whatever they want to do – with that
very unusual tusk!

After You Read

1. The beluga whale is _____ very social animal.
    A. the
    B. an
    C. that
    D. a

2. An adult beluga whale is grey.
    A. True
    B. False
    C. Not in text

3. On page 7, 'it' in the phrase 'It can't get back to the water' refers to:
    A. the shore
    B. a baby beluga
    C. the ocean
    D. deeper water

4. What is a good heading for page 8?
    A. Young Whale in Trouble
    B. Mother and Calf Swim Together
    C. Adult Beluga Makes Deadly Mistake
    D. Whale Finds New Home

5. After the tide comes back, where does the young whale go?
    A. to the rocks
    B. to the other whales
    C. to the shore
    D. to the ice

6. What is the purpose of a narwhal's tusk?
    A. to break ice
    B. to swim better
    C. to look for codfish
    D. to sense the temperature

7. The purpose of page 12 is:
    A. to describe belugas.
    B. to describe all the whales living in the Arctic Ocean.
    C. to describe a beluga's tusk.
    D. to explain what makes narwhals special.

8. On page 15, 'a big risk' means:
    A. something good
    B. something unusual
    C. something bad might happen
    D. something great

9. The narwhals are trapped in the _____.
    A. shore
    B. rocks
    C. open sea
    D. bay

10. The writer thinks that belugas and narwhals are interesting because:
    A. they sometimes get into trouble.
    B. they are not social animals.
    C. they don't swim well.
    D. they argue with each other.

11. According to the story, which of the following is true for belugas and narwhals?
    A. They have tusks.
    B. They change colour as they grow.
    C. They never get into trouble.
    D. They breathe oxygen.

Visiting
the Arctic

You've seen pictures of beluga whales and narwhals. You've read about how they live in the Arctic Ocean. But have you ever thought of visiting the Arctic yourself? Every year thousands of people do. They get there on ships that leave from cities in Canada, Russia, and parts of Europe. Here are some questions that people planning a trip to the Arctic often ask.

Tourists on a ship in the Arctic Ocean

Q: WHAT KINDS OF SHIPS GO TO THE ARCTIC?

A: Only special ships can go to the Arctic. They must be very strong because of all the ice in the Arctic Ocean. Many of the ships are also quite small. The largest ones hold no more than 100 people. Most of them hold around 50 people. Some ships leave from small towns in northern Canada. Tourists usually have to fly there from Montreal. People can also leave from cities in northern Europe or the northern part of Russia.

Q: WHEN IS THE BEST TIME TO GO?

A: The best time to visit the Arctic Ocean is during the months of July and August. During these months, the temperatures are usually above 45 degrees Fahrenheit (7 degrees Celsius) during the day. In January and February, the temperature can be very cold. During these months, ice covers many parts of the Arctic Ocean and ships cannot pass through. In some places this ice can be several feet thick.

'Most travellers say that their trip to the Arctic was very interesting.'

Q: WHAT DO PEOPLE DO ON THE SHIP?

A: Most ships offer classes every day. People can learn about the things they will see on shore. They can also learn about the history of the area. Who first found the area? What did they see there? There are also often classes about local sea animals, like birds, whales, or codfish. All of these animals are common in the Arctic. Most travellers say that their trip to the Arctic was very interesting. Some think it's the best vacation they've ever taken.

Word Count: 316
Time: _____

Words to Know

This story is set in Niger, which is a country in Africa. It happens in the Sahara Desert.

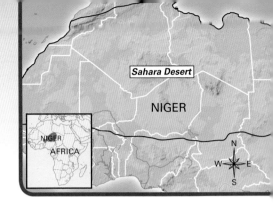

Sahara Desert

NIGER

NIGER

AFRICA

N
W—E
S

A **Parts of a Dinosaur.** Read the sentences. Write the number of the correct <u>underlined</u> word next to each item in the picture.

1. The <u>shoulder girdle</u> joins the body and the arms or front legs.
2. The <u>pelvis</u> joins the body and the back legs.
3. The <u>limbs</u> are the arms and legs of a body.
4. The <u>jaw</u> is the lower part of the face that moves when the mouth opens.

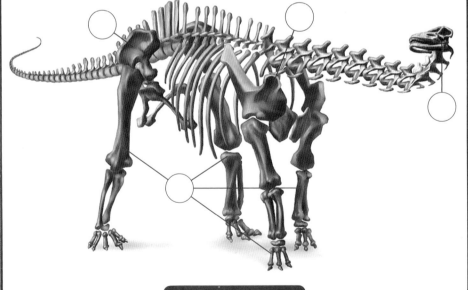

A Dinosaur Skeleton

B **Fossils in the Desert.** Look at the pictures and read the paragraph. Then complete the paragraph with the words in the box.

bones	fossils	prehistoric
desert	palaeontologists	sand

Dinosaurs are (1)_____ animals. They lived long before people documented history. The scientists who study them are called (2)_____. These scientists often study dinosaur (3)_____, or the hard parts inside the body. They also study animal and plant parts that have been saved in rock. These are called (4)_____. In this story, a team of scientists looks for dinosaur parts in the (5)_____. The dry air there helps save the dinosaur bones. However, sometimes the (6)_____ covers up the bones so they are difficult to find.

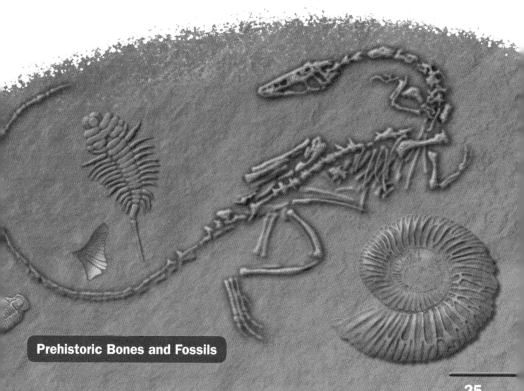

Prehistoric Bones and Fossils

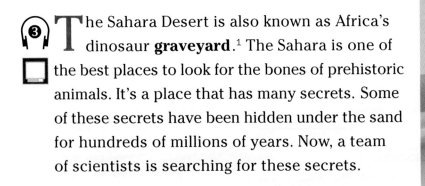

The Sahara Desert is also known as Africa's dinosaur **graveyard**.[1] The Sahara is one of the best places to look for the bones of prehistoric animals. It's a place that has many secrets. Some of these secrets have been hidden under the sand for hundreds of millions of years. Now, a team of scientists is searching for these secrets.

---

[1]**graveyard:** an area of land where dead bodies are buried

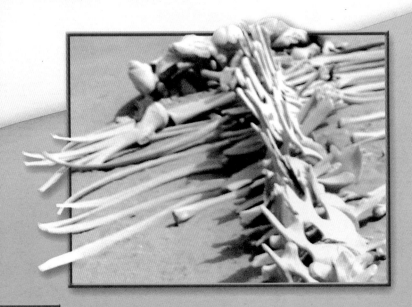

Palaeontologist[1] Dr Paul Sereno and his team are in the Sahara looking for **clues**.[2] They hope that these clues will lead them to dinosaur bones. These bones may help them to better understand dinosaurs and the time period in which they lived. Dr Sereno explains: 'We're **on the trail of**[3] a number of dinosaurs. We begin to **paint a much better picture**[4] of this time [period] each time we come [to the Sahara].'

The team drives across the desert. Then suddenly, one of the team members says, 'Hey! Back there!' The team stops to look around the area. They're near the right place!

---

[1]**palaeontologist:** sb who studies the ancient history of the earth using fossils
[2]**clue:** a sign that helps to solve a problem or answer a question
[3]**on the trail of:** following; trying to find
[4]**paint a better picture (of sth):** make sth easier to understand

Dr Sereno first discovered **fossils**[1] in the Sahara when he was travelling there in 1997. Since then, he's been carefully planning more visits. But planning this kind of travel isn't easy. The team has to worry about the weather and other planning problems. Methods of travel, the team's safety, and the timing of the visit are all very important issues to consider.

After a lot of hard work, Dr Sereno and his team have made it back to Niger. They have returned to the Sahara at last. They have now reached a place far from the rest of the world – the dinosaur graveyard that Dr Sereno visited years before.

---

[1] **fossil:** sth from an ancient animal or plant, such as a bone, feather, footprint, or leaf, that has been saved in rocks

Scan for Information

Scan page 30 to find the information.

1. When did Dr Sereno first discover fossils in the Sahara Desert?

2. What problems do Dr Sereno and his team have when visiting the Sahara Desert?

3. Where is the team now?

Now that the team is in the correct place, the dinosaur search can begin. There are bones everywhere in this dinosaur graveyard.

It doesn't take the team a long time to discover them. They talk about the bones as they find them. 'It's part of a **shoulder girdle**,'[1] says one team member, as he picks up a bone. Another team member finds something else. 'It's a **distal end**[2] of a limb bone right there,' he says as he points to the end of a bone. And another: 'We've got what looks like a leg.'

Nearby, there's another discovery. 'Hey look at this!' says one member. 'It's a **pelvis**!'[3] However, as another team member comes closer to see the bone, he gets in trouble. 'Wait, you're stepping on it!' says the team member who found it. Everyone needs to be very careful with these prehistoric bones and fossils!

---

[1] **shoulder girdle:** bones where the arms connect to the body
[2] **distal end:** part farthest away from where sth is attached
[3] **pelvis:** bones where the legs connect to the lower back

The dinosaur search continues. The team finds bones from several prehistoric animals. They have collected a lot of **promising**[1] fossils, and are very happy about it. Unfortunately, life isn't so good for the team in other ways.

The desert is a hot place, and the team has **used up**[2] most of their water. They are now worried because the water **truck**[3] hasn't arrived yet. 'After today, we'll have a day and a half's worth of water,' says one team member. 'We're just hoping for the water truck to get here in time,' he adds. Luckily, it does!

Their water worries are over, and there's one more thing they don't have to worry about …

---

[1] **promising:** likely to be very good or helpful in the future
[2] **used up:** use sth which has only a limited supply
[3] **truck:** lorry

… and that's finding enough fossils! The team makes one important discovery after another. They carefully document each find.

Then, one day as they are walking around, they make their biggest discovery yet; they find the jaw of the prehistoric crocodile sometimes called 'super croc'! This discovery is big – very big – and the jaw bone is in very good condition.

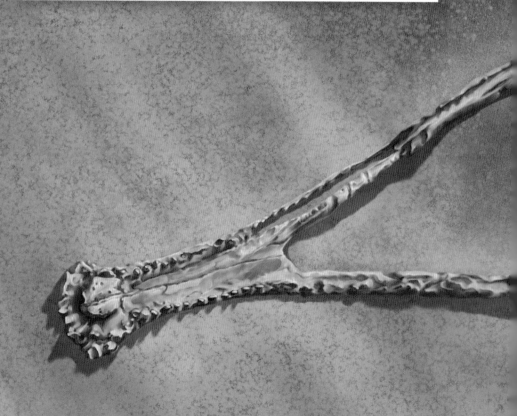

The palaeontologists make a big discovery.

Length: 12 metres
Weight: 9,000 kilograms

Prehistoric Super Croc

Today's Nile Crocodile

Length: 5 metres
Weight: 225 kilograms

In fact, the discovery of the **jaw bone**[1] is so important that the team soon gets a visit. National Geographic crocodile expert Brady Barr comes to the work site. Barr looks at the super croc bones with Dr Sereno as they talk about the super croc. This ancient animal was very, very large. It was far bigger than the crocodiles that live today. The questions that scientists have about super croc are big too. What did it look like? What did it eat? How did it hunt?

---

[1]**jaw bone:** the bones of the mouth

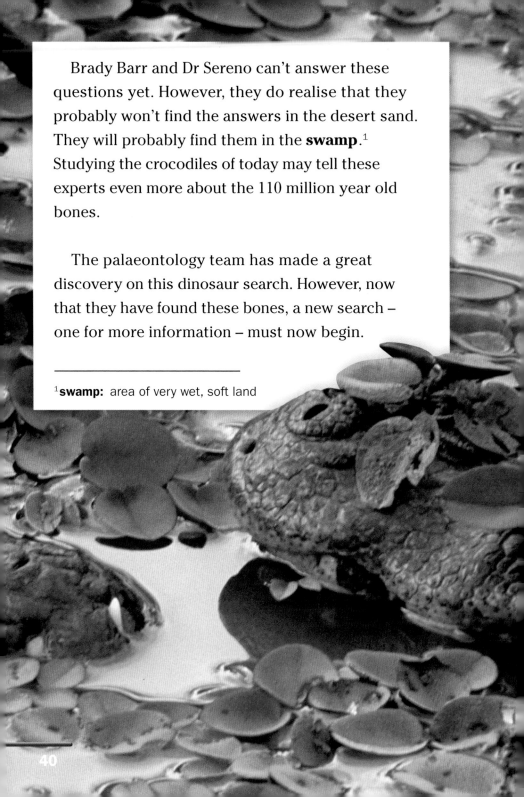

Brady Barr and Dr Sereno can't answer these questions yet. However, they do realise that they probably won't find the answers in the desert sand. They will probably find them in the **swamp**.[1] Studying the crocodiles of today may tell these experts even more about the 110 million year old bones.

The palaeontology team has made a great discovery on this dinosaur search. However, now that they have found these bones, a new search – one for more information – must now begin.

---

[1]**swamp:** area of very wet, soft land

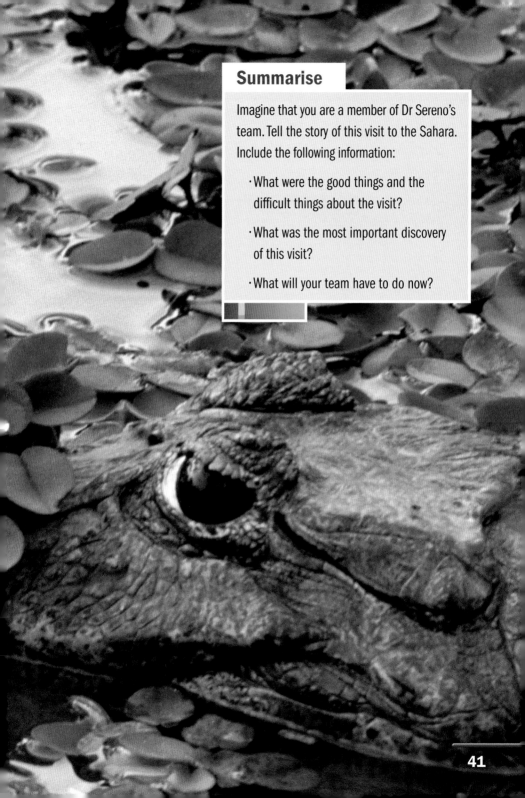

Summarise

Imagine that you are a member of Dr Sereno's team. Tell the story of this visit to the Sahara. Include the following information:

- What were the good things and the difficult things about the visit?

- What was the most important discovery of this visit?

- What will your team have to do now?

After You Read

1. On page 26, the word 'team' can be replaced by:
    A. test
    B. researchers
    C. group
    D. class

2. In the Sahara Desert, secrets have been hidden _____ many years.
    A. while
    B. for
    C. in
    D. under

3. On page 29, 'them' in 'will lead them' refers to:
    A. bones
    B. clues
    C. dinosaurs
    D. palaeontologists

4. Dr. Sereno thinks the bones can teach us about:
    A. painting.
    B. history.
    C. trails.
    D. palaeontologists.

5. Weather, safety, and timing are all important considerations for the team's visit.
    A. True
    B. False

6. What is a good heading for the second paragraph on page 30?
    A. Team Arrives at Fossil Site
    B. Graveyard Close to Home
    C. Sereno Comes Often to Visit
    D. Team Leaves the Sahara

7. What's the main purpose of page 33?
   A. to show that the team is unsure about the bones
   B. to show that the team is never careful
   C. to show that there are many different types of dinosaur bones
   D. to teach about different kinds of fossils

8. The best heading for page 34 is:
   A. Team Only Has Success.
   B. Team Has Success but Faces Problems.
   C. Only Problems with Visit.
   D. Water Never Arrives.

9. The team uses_____ all of their water.
   A. just
   B. almost
   C. might
   D. maybe

10. On page 36, the verb 'document' means:
   A. to record
   B. to think
   C. to refer
   D. to decide

11. What is significant about the super croc discovery?
   A. the importance of the discovery
   B. the size of the fossil
   C. the good condition of the fossil
   D. all of the above

12. Why is the answer in the swamp?
   A. Because the sand is too deep.
   B. Because the swamp is very old.
   C. Because they must study living crocodiles.
   D. Because the rest of the bones are there.

DINOSAUR Discoveries

Dinosaur Eggs

Palaeontologists know that dinosaurs grew and developed inside eggs. These eggs were hard and they protected the young dinosaurs. The process is similar to how birds grow and develop nowadays. However, dinosaur eggs are different from bird eggs. The outside of a dinosaur egg is much heavier. Dinosaur eggs are also a lot bigger than bird eggs. Dinosaurs created special places to keep their eggs safe and warm called 'nests'. Birds also build nests for their eggs. Most birds build their nests in trees. However, prehistoric dinosaurs built their nests on the ground. Interestingly, palaeontologists think that dinosaurs covered their nests with dead plants to keep the eggs warm. A few of today's birds also do this.

Dinosaur Eggs

Dinosaur Footprints

Dinosaur footprints range in size – some are very small and some are very large. These footprints were made millions of years ago when the ground was soft and wet. Later on, sand filled the footprints. As time passed, this earth and sand turned into stone and the footprints remained in the stone. Nowadays, palaeontologists can tell a lot from dinosaur footprints. For example, the depth of the footprint helps them to understand how heavy the dinosaur was. Recently, palaeontologists have discovered lots of footprints going in the same direction. This means that dinosaurs probably travelled together in large groups.

Dinosaur Footprints

Dinosaur Fossils

The best dinosaur fossils were formed when three things happened in a very short period of time. First, the dinosaur died. After that, the soft parts of the dinosaur went into the earth. The dinosaur bones remained on the ground. Finally, the bones and dinosaur parts were covered by sand before any were lost or broken. Palaeontologists study fossils to learn about dinosaurs. They are always searching for new fossils. However, it is not always easy to find them. Fossils are usually discovered in two ways. Sometimes the wind wears the earth away. This makes it easier for palaeontologists to spot new fossils. Other times fossils are uncovered by workers preparing to build a new road or building.

Word Count: 335
Time: _____

Words to Know

This story is set in the United States (U.S.). It happens in the state of Maryland, in a city called Baltimore.

Baltimore
Maryland

CANADA
UNITED STATES
Maryland
MEXICO

A **Elephants in the Wild.** Read the facts about elephants. Then write each underlined word or phrase next to the correct definition.

When elephants are in the wild, they are free.
Elephants live in families, like humans do.
Several elephant families often come together to make a herd.
When it is hot, elephants like to get into water and mud.
Elephants use their trunks to pick things up.

1. a soft combination of water and earth: _____

2. people: _____

3. the long powerful nose of an elephant: _____

4. in natural conditions: _____

5. a large group of animals of the same type that live and eat together: _____

A Herd of Elephants

B **Elephants at Work.** Look at the pictures and read the paragraph. Then complete the paragraph with the words in the box.

| gentle | captivity | trainer | circus | zoo |

If elephants aren't in the wild, they are usually in (1) _____ and are kept by people. These elephants often live in a zoo or work in a circus. A (2) _____ is a place where many animals live and people can go to see them. Many people love elephants because they're usually very friendly and (3) _____. Other elephants work in a (4) _____. This is a kind of show in which people and animals perform. An animal (5) _____ works with these elephants. This person teaches the elephants what to do in the show.

An Elephant in the Zoo

An Animal Trainer with a Circus Elephant

Elephants are very large animals, but they are also very gentle. They are important to humans too. Elephants and people have worked together for over 2,000 years. However, when they work with humans, the elephants are not usually in the wild. They are usually in captivity and working in zoos or circuses.

During these 2,000 years, people have learnt a lot about the way elephants act. However, there is one question that people are still concerned about: How can people keep elephants happy when they are in captivity?

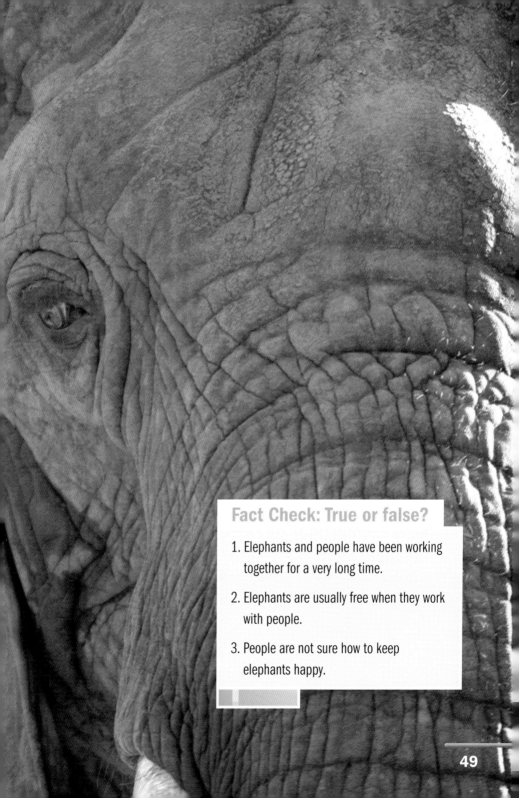

Fact Check: True or false?

1. Elephants and people have been working together for a very long time.

2. Elephants are usually free when they work with people.

3. People are not sure how to keep elephants happy.

Mike Hackenberger is a skilled animal trainer at Baltimore Zoo. He works hard to make sure his elephants are healthy and seem happy. His elephants even seem to say 'hello' when Hackenberger says, 'OK, everyone, trunk-foot **salute**!'[1]

'We make sure teeth are where they're supposed to be, [they] don't have **ingrown feet**[2] … ' he explains. 'This is all that good **husbandry**[3] stuff,' he adds. Hackenberger is responsible for teaching other zoo workers how to recognise a happy elephant. Part of his method for doing this is to talk to the elephants. 'Oh you're happy … ' he says to one elephant. 'Hear that?' he asks as the elephant makes a low noise, 'That's a happy sound,' he reports. 'That's a good sound.'

---

[1] **salute:** an action or gesture to show respect to sb
[2] **ingrown feet:** an uncomfortable condition of the foot
[3] **husbandry:** animal care

A Trunk-Foot Salute

But can elephants really be happy? Do animals have feelings? If so, are their feelings the same as people's feelings? There's a big discussion about this subject. Many people who work closely with animals say that they do have feelings and can experience happiness. These people think animals are just like humans. Other people are not so certain.

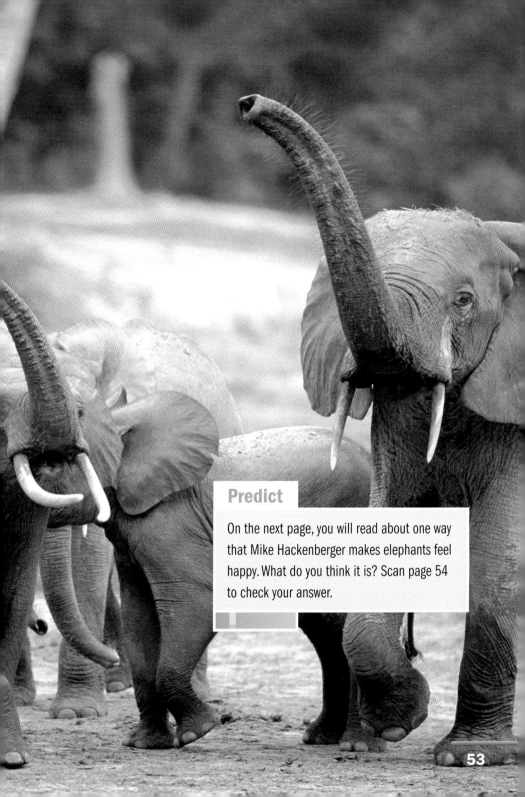

Predict

On the next page, you will read about one way that Mike Hackenberger makes elephants feel happy. What do you think it is? Scan page 54 to check your answer.

There is one thing that everyone agrees on when they talk about elephants. Elephants seem happier – and safer – if their home in the zoo or circus is very similar to their life among their **herd**[1] in the wild. Today, zoos work hard to make elephants **feel** as '**at home**'[2] as possible.

Hackenberger also talks to the elephants, and this may help to make them feel better. 'Head over, let's go kids,' he says to a group of elephants. 'Let's go, Fatman! Let's go … watch yourself,' he says with a smile. He also encourages the animals as they move along, 'We're walking, guys. Come on, Funnyface, good boy,' he says.

---

[1]**herd:** a large group of animals
[2]**feel at home:** feel relaxed and comfortable

According to Hackenberger, elephant training has improved in recent years. He explains, 'I'll tell you … 10, 15, 25 years ago, some of the **techniques**[1] were a bit **barbaric**.[2] We've **walked away from**[3] that … society's walked away from [treating animals like that].' That's news that makes everybody happy.

---

[1]**technique:** a way of doing something that needs skill
[2]**barbaric:** very unkind
[3]**walk away from:** leave behind

One important fact about elephants is that they are social animals. This means that they usually live in families and herds. They need other elephants. Therefore, if they are alone for a long time, they seem to be unhappy and they can start to act in an unusual way.

Hackenberger talks about one elephant, called Limba. Limba was alone for 30 years in a zoo in northern **Quebec**,[1] and she was not very happy by herself. Hackenberger then tells the story of how two other elephants came to live with Limba. They were only two days old at the time. He thinks Limba 'fell in love' with the two young elephants. He also feels that is the reason Limba became happier, and more like a normal elephant.

_____

[1]**Quebec:** a part of Canada

Limba fell in love with the two young elephants.

When he is training elephants, Hackenberger talks to them a lot. He's very gentle with them as well. Most importantly, he lets them do the things that they do when they are free in the wild.

For example, elephants love to swim and play in the mud. 'Do you … you want to go swimming?' Hackenberger asks the elephants. '**Absolutely**,'[1] he answers for one of them as the elephant actually **nods his head**![2] 'Let's get in the water,' he says and takes them to the mud hole. The animals really seem to like this pleasant activity.

---

[1]**absolutely:** yes(!); of course(!)
[2]**nod (one's) head:** move one's head up and down to say yes

So what is the answer to the question: How can people keep elephants happy when they are **in captivity**?[1] For Hackenberger, the answer is not difficult. He believes that elephants need to learn how to be elephants, just as they are in the wild.

'Are they trained?' he asks a person visiting the zoo. 'I think so,' she replies. 'They're trained to be elephants!' he explains. He then tells one of his very large friends, 'Just be an elephant!' With Hackenberger's help, it certainly seems as though his animals are very, very happy elephants!

---

[1]**in captivity:** be kept as a prisoner

Summarise

What does Hackenberger think about how to keep elephants happy? Summarise this in one sentence.

After You Read

1. On page 48, the word 'gentle' in the first paragraph means:
   A. active
   B. funny
   C. wild
   D. kind

2. There is one question about elephants that people _____ agree on: Can elephants be happy?
   A. will
   B. cannot
   C. do
   D. can

3. Hackenberger tries to make his elephants happy by talking to them.
   A. True
   B. False

4. A good heading for page 50 is:
   A. Man Trains Elephants to Make Happy Sounds.
   B. Trainer and Elephants Happy at Seattle Zoo.
   C. Trainer Talks to Elephants Too Much.
   D. Elephants Are Happy with Caring Trainer.

5. Most people who work with animals think that animals have feelings.
   A. True
   B. False

6. On page 52, who is 'they'?
   A. trainers
   B. feelings
   C. animals
   D. people

7. Society has walked away from _____ animal training techniques.
   A. easy
   B. unkind
   C. good
   D. any

8. What is the meaning of 'unusual' on page 58?
   A. good
   B. happy
   C. boring
   D. strange

9. Limba fell in love with the young elephants because:
   A. elephants love all children.
   B. elephants are social animals.
   C. young elephants are good trainers.
   D. elephants enjoy living alone.

10. Which of the following is something elephants do in the wild?
    A. swim and play in the mud
    B. communicate with people
    C. play with trainers
    D. live alone

11. What does Hackenberger believe about making elephants happy in captivity?
    A. Elephants can't be happy in a zoo.
    B. Elephants are happy anywhere they can be elephants.
    C. Elephants are happy in captivity if they have a good trainer.
    D. Elephants are happiest when they are alone.

Be an Elephant Keeper

Every year thousands of young people leave school for a few weeks or months and enjoy an unusual type of educational programme. What they learn during this time does not come from books. They learn new skills by living in a different country and doing unusual jobs. There are several organisations that help students to find the experience they are looking for. The job description table below shows a few possibilities for students.

Country	Job	Time	Description
India	Teaching young children	Two months	• Teach music and art • Help children to learn how to communicate
Ghana	Health care worker	Three months	• See how doctors work in a less developed country • Help care for some people
Thailand	Saving elephants	Three weeks	• Cleaning elephants • Helping train elephants

A job can be a learning experience.

Students help to clean the elephants.

One interesting possibility is helping elephants in Thailand. Most people think of elephants as animals in zoos or circuses. However, many elephants in Thailand are no longer kept in captivity. Now, hundreds of them are homeless. These gentle animals are often found on the streets as they do not have owners to care for them. Although they may look well, they are often in poor health and don't have enough to eat.

One centre in Thailand cares for these elephants. It provides a safe and natural living space for them. When they are at the centre, they stay in a building but are free to walk around. Students come from all over the world to help here. The student helpers work with the elephant keepers. These keepers train the students in caring for the elephants. In the morning, they go to the forest together and lead the elephants to the centre. They clean them and give them food. In the afternoon, they take the animals back into the forest for the night. Helping at the centre is interesting and the young people learn a lot.

Word Count: 321
Time: _____

Grammar Focus: Present Perfect

■ The present perfect is formed by the auxiliary *have/has* + the 3rd form (past participle).

■ The present perfect is used:
  1. for actions at an unspecified time in the past
  2. for things that happened several times in the past
  3. for actions that started at a specified time in the past and continue now.

I		
You	have	
We	haven't	done the homework.
They		seen that movie.
		taken the test.
He	has	finished that book.
She	hasn't	

Grammar Practice: Present Perfect

Have you done these things today? Write sentences with the present perfect tense.

e.g. eat lunch   *I've eaten lunch. / I haven't eaten lunch yet.*

1. finish your homework _____

2. take a shower   _____

3. go to English class   _____

4. check your e-mail   _____

5. (your own idea)   _____

Grammar Focus: Present Perfect Question Forms

| Have | you
we
they | (ever) been late to class?
(ever) seen that movie?
finished the book? | Yes, I have.
No, I haven't. |
| Has | he
she | taken the test? | Yes, he has.
No, he hasn't. |

Grammar Practice: Present Perfect Question Forms

Write questions and answers about these things with the present perfect tense. Write true answers.

e.g. you/live in
a big city

Have you ever lived in a big city?
Yes, I have. OR No, I haven't.

6. you/see
a whale

_____

_____

7. you/be
in danger

_____

_____

8. you/take a trip
on a boat

_____

_____

9. you/go to a zoo

_____

_____

Grammar Focus: Past Continuous

- The past continuous is formed with the past tense of *be* and the present participle (-ing) form of the main verb.

- The past continuous is used:
    1. for actions in progress at a specific point in the past
    2. for two or more actions in progress over the same time period in the past

In 1997	Dr Sereno	was looking for fossils in the Sahara Desert.	
At 7:00	Betsy and Lou	were studying at the university.	
	Our teacher	was living in Bangkok	in 1997.
	I	was making soup	at 7:00.

Grammar Practice: Past Continuous

Write questions with the past continuous tense.

e.g. 7:00 last night/Mike/wash the dishes
At 7:00 last night Mike was washing the dishes.

1. 6:30 a.m./I/take a shower
   _____

2. Thursday afternoon/you/writing email messages
   _____

3. 9:00 yesterday morning/the students/study English
   _____

4. 2005/Ms. Brown/teach in Europe
   _____

Grammar Focus: Past Continuous with When and While

■ The past continuous can be used with *when* and a clause in the simple past tense to show that something was in progress when another event happened.

■ The past continuous can be used with *while* and another clause in the past continuous to show that two things were in progress at the same time in the past.

Grammar Practice: Past Continuous with When and While

Circle the correct ending for each sentence.

e.g. We were reading newspapers in the house while
       a. it was raining outside.
       b. my friend said 'hello'.

5. He was eating lunch when
       a. his friends were taking pictures.
       b. he saw his friend.

6. They were travelling in Australia when
       a. they found the dinosaur bones.
       b. they were meeting each other.

7. Lillian was climbing a mountain while
       a. Kyle was sightseeing.
       b. she broke her leg bone.

8. What were you doing while
       a. I was talking on the telephone?
       b. I lost my notebook?

Grammar Focus: Imperatives

■ Make the imperative with the base form of the verb.
Make negative imperatives with *don't*.

■ Use the imperative to give an order or to give instructions.

■ Use *please* to make imperatives more polite: *Please be quiet.*
Please don't be noisy.

Imperatives	Negative Imperatives
<u>Be</u> quiet.	<u>Don't be</u> noisy.
<u>Speak</u> English.	<u>Don't speak</u> Chinese.
<u>Eat</u> fruit.	<u>Don't eat</u> ice cream.

Grammar Practice: Imperatives
A. Read the zoo rules and write imperative sentences.

✗	Give food to animals.
✓	Read information signs
✗	Touch animals
✓	Put papers in garbage cans
✗	Put hands in cages

e.g. *Don't give food to the animals.*

1. _____

2. _____

3. _____

4. _____

Grammar Practice: Imperatives

B. Write instructions for elephant trainers with imperatives. Use your own ideas.

e.g. _Give the elephant his favourite food every day._

5. _____

6. _____

7. _____

8. _____

9. _____

10. _____

Video Practice

A. Watch the video of *Arctic Whale Danger!* and choose the main idea.
   1. Life isn't always easy for whales.
   2. Whales are in danger from people.
   3. Whales can be very dangerous for ships.

B. Read the sentences. Then watch the video again and circle the word you hear.
   1. 'A mother and her calf will often swim together for (two/three) years.'
   2. 'It can't get back to the (ocean/water).'
   3. 'The other belugas can only watch as the calf tries to (swim/move).'
   4. 'And finally it's free again, and is able to (return/go back) to the water.'
   5. 'Perhaps it has learned something from this (scary/bad) experience.'

C. Watch the video again and answer the questions. Write complete sentences.
   1. Where do narwhals live?
   2. How long can a narwhal's tusk grow?
   3. How many narwhals are in the group today?
   4. What do the narwhals want to eat?
   5. What do narwhals breathe?

   1. _____

   2. _____

   3. _____

   4. _____

   5. _____

D. Watch the video of *Dinosaur Search* and write True or False.

1. There are no plants in the Sahara Desert. _____
2. The scientists want to paint pictures of dinosaurs. _____
3. Since 1997, Dr. Sereno has wanted to return to the desert. _____
4. It is easy to drive in the Sahara Desert. _____
5. One of the scientists steps on a dinosaur bone. _____

E. Watch the video again and write the word or words you hear.

1. 'The team finds bones from several _____ animals … '
2. 'We're just hoping for the _____ to get here in time.'
3. 'They carefully document each _____.'
4. 'This ancient animal was very, very _____.'
5. 'The _____ has made a great discovery.'

F. Watch the video of *Happy Elephants* and circle the main idea.

1. Elephants are happier in the wild.
2. People and elephants have been together for a long time.
3. Elephant trainers try to find ways to make elephants happier.

G. Watch the video again. Circle the correct word in parentheses for each of the five questions below.

1. 'Elephants are very large but they are (friendly/gentle) and intelligent animals.'
2. 'Elephants and people have (worked/lived) together for over 2,000 years.'
3. 'How can people keep elephants happy in (the zoo/captivity)?'
4. 'His elephants are very (active/healthy) and seem to be happy.'
5. 'Many people who work closely with (animals/elephants) say that they do have feelings and can experience happiness.'

(1) Narwhals do not look like beluga whales. **(2)** Narwhals have a long tusk or horn. **(3)** It's almost like a tooth. **(4)** It grows out of the whale's top lip. **(5)** They don't use the tusk to eat. **(6)** However, sometimes they use it to fight. **(7)** Narwhals don't usually swim alone. **(8)** They often eat codfish. **(9)** They need to breathe air to live. **(10)** If they swim under ice and can't get air, they will die.

1. The writer thinks that narwhals _____.
   A. like to be alone
   B. are interesting
   C. like to be with people
   D. are not clean

2. What is a good heading for this paragraph?
   A. Narwhals and Belugas
   B. What Do Narwhals Eat?
   C. Why Narwhals Have Tusks
   D. An Introduction to Narwhals

3. In sentence 4 the word 'it' refers to _____.
   A. a baby narwhal
   B. a fight
   C. a tooth
   D. a narwhal's tusk

4. Where should this sentence go?
   They move around in small groups.
   A. after sentence 4
   B. after sentence 7
   C. after sentence 9
   D. after sentence 2

5. Narwhals use their tusks to _____.
  A. eat
  B. swim
  C. fight
  D. breathe

6. According to the paragraph, which of the following sentences is NOT true?
  A. Narwhals breathe air.
  B. Narwhals eat codfish.
  C. Narwhals use their tusks to fight.
  D. Narwhals look like Beluga whales.

7. A bay is _____.
  A. part of a whale's body
  B. another word for 'ocean'
  C. the same as a 'tide'
  D. a part of the sea that is nearly closed in by land

8. The students _____ a video about beluga whales.
  A. has seen
  B. are seen
  C. have seen
  D. seed

9. She _____ on a whale watch yet.
  A. hasn't been
  B. didn't have been
  C. not has been
  D. haven't been

10. Ice is _____.
  A. another word for 'tusk'
  B. another word for 'shore'
  C. hard pieces of water formed in the cold
  D. the same as water

(1) The Sahara Desert in Africa is one of the best places in the world to look for dinosaur bones. **(2)** Dr. Paul Sereno first discovered fossils there in 1997 and now he is going back again. **(3)** It takes a long time to plan one of these trips. **(4)** Dr. Sereno has to think about the weather, methods of travel, and safety. **(5)** He and his team of palaeontologists have returned to the place where he found so many dinosaur bones in the past. **(6)** They have no problem finding bones. **(7)** But they do have a different problem. **(8)** They have very little water left. **(9)** The water truck is late. **(10)** They have only about enough water for a day and a half. **(11)** But then the truck arrives and all is well. **(12)** And soon they find something very unusual in the sand. **(13)** They discover the jaw bone of a very large crocodile called a 'super croc'. **(14)** This is their biggest discovery yet.

A. Read the paragraph and answer the questions.

11. The Sahara Desert _____.
    A. is the only place in the world with dinosaur fossils
    B. is a place where Dr Sereno has discovered fossils in the past
    C. does not have many dinosaur bones
    D. has a good supply of water for the scientists

12. Trips like this one _____.
    A. are not expensive
    B. are very dangerous
    C. require a lot of planning
    D. are very common

13. The team becomes worried because _____.
    A. the water truck is late
    B. the weather is bad
    C. they find crocodile bones, not dinosaur bones
    D. they don't feel safe

14. Where does this sentence go?
In the Sahara there are many secrets hidden under the sand.
  A. after sentence 1
  B. after sentence 4
  C. after sentence 8
  D. after sentence 9

15. The word 'they' in sentence 7 refers to _____.
  A. the methods of travel
  B. Dr Sereno and the palaeontologists
  C. the trips
  D. the dinosaur bones

16. A good title for this paragraph is _____.
  A. Weather and Safety Problems Make Life Difficult
  B. Dr Sereno and His Team Plan a Trip to the Sahara Desert
  C. Dr Sereno and His Team Find Water in the Desert
  D. Palaeontologists Face Problems but Make an Important
    Discovery

17. The jaw is part of the _____ of an animal.
  A. face   **C.** pelvis
  B. shoulder   **D.** leg

18. The hard parts inside an animal's body are called _____.
  A. fossils   **C.** limbs
  B. sand   **D.** bones

19. What _____ to find in the desert?
  A. Dr Sereno was trying
  B. was Dr Sereno trying
  C. did Dr Sereno trying
  D. did Dr Sereno tried

20. The palaeontologists _____ across the desert when they
discovered the dinosaur graveyard.
  A. are driving   **C.** were driving
  B. were drove   **D.** are driven

(1) Two things are very important to elephants – communication and social relationships. (2) In that way, they are no different from humans. (3) Therefore, most elephant trainers talk to their animals a lot when they work with them. (4) Many trainers also let the elephants do things they like to do in the wild. (5) For example, they let them swim and play together in the mud. (6) One trainer, Mike Hackenberger, even gives names to the elephants he works with. (7) This is just one more way that he uses to open communication and build social relationships with these large animals.

21. According to the paragraph, which statement is true?
    A. Mike Hackenberger owns several elephants.
    B. Mike Hackenberger is not gentle with the elephants.
    C. Mike Hackenberger cares about elephants' feelings.
    D. Mike Hackenberger works with elephants in wild.

22. Elephants _____.
    A. don't like to be alone
    B. don't like humans
    C. don't like mud
    D. don't like swimming

23. Communication is important to elephants. Therefore, _____.
    A. some trainers only feed them once a day
    B. some trainers talk to them
    C. some trainers keep them in captivity
    D. some trainers don't give them names

24. Where should this sentence go?
    He calls one of them 'Fatman'.
    A. after sentence 2   **C.** after sentence 6
    B. after sentence 4   **D.** after sentence 8

25. In sentence 2 the word 'they' refers to _____.
    A. humans   **C.** elephant trainers
    B. social relationships   **D.** elephants

26. The purpose of the paragraph is to _____.
    A. show that elephants are not always friendly

B. show that elephants should stay in the wild
C. show how elephants and humans are similar
D. show what trainers should not do

27. The word 'gentle' is similar to the word _____.
    A. unhappy   **C.** wild
    B. large   **D.** quiet

28. Choose the correct verb form.
    The teacher often tells her students, '_____
    your dictionary.'
    A. Not to forget   **C.** Don't forget
    B. Not forget   **D.** Not forgetting

29. Elephants always live in a herd when they are _____.
    A. in the wild
    B. in captivity
    C. in a circus
    D. in a zoo

30. Choose the correct sentence.
    At the beginning of class, the teacher says, '_____.'
    A. Let's begin now
    B. Let's beginning now
    C. Let's to begin now
    D. Let's began now

Key 答案

Arctic Whale Danger!
Words to Know: A. 1. shore **2.** beluga whale **3.** ice **4.** rocks **5.** bay
6. narwhal **B. 1.** Beluga whales **2.** Narwhals **3.** calf **4.** codfish
Reading Skills Boxes: Predict: The beluga calf will be OK because the water will come back.
Fact Check: 1. They have a long tusk. **2.** They were looking for codfish.
3. It closed the opening to the sea. **4.** The narwhals are trapped.
After You Read: 1. D **2.** B **3.** B **4.** A **5.** B **6.** D **7.** D **8.** C **9.** D **10.** A **11.** D

Dinosaur Search
Words to Know: A. (from left to right) **2** (pelvis) **3** (limbs) **1** (shoulder girdle) **4** (jaw) **B. 1.** prehistoric **2.** palaeontologists **3.** bones **4.** fossils **5.** desert **6.** sand
Reading Skills Boxes:
Scan for Information: 1. in 1997 **2.** weather, methods of travel, safety, and timing of the visit **3.** in the Sahara Desert in Africa
Summarise:
(suggested answer) Our visit to the Sahara was a good visit because we found many fossils, but we were worried about the water truck arriving in time. Finding the bones of the 'super croc' was the most important discovery. Now our team will have to study modern crocodiles to find out more information.
After You Read: 1. C **2.** B **3.** D **4.** B **5.** A **6.** A **7.** C **8.** B **9.** B **10.** A **11.** D **12.** C

Happy Elephants
Words to Know: A. 1. mud **2.** humans **3.** trunk **4.** in the wild **5.** herd
B. 1. captivity **2.** zoo **3.** gentle **4.** circus **5.** trainer
Reading Skills Boxes
Fact Check: 1. True **2.** False **3.** True
Predict: He talks to the elephants.
Summarise:
Mike Hackenberger thinks that elephants in captivity need to learn how to live like elephants in the wild and play and be social together.
After You Read: 1. D **2.** B **3.** A **4.** D **5.** A **6.** C **7.** B **8.** D **9.** B **10.** A **11.** B

Grammar Practice
Present Perfect:
1. I've finished my homework./I haven't finished my homework.
2. I've taken a shower./I haven't taken a shower.
3. I've gone to English class./I haven't gone to English class.
4. I've checked my e-mail./I haven't checked my e-mail.
5. Open answers.
6. Have you ever seen a whale? Yes, I have./No, I haven't.
7. Have you ever been in danger? Yes, I have./No, I haven't.
8. Have you ever taken a trip on a boat? Yes, I have./No, I haven't.
9. Have you ever gone to a zoo? Yes, I have./No, I haven't.

Past Continuous:
1. At 6:30 a.m. I was taking a shower. **2.** On Thursday afternoon you were writing e-mail messages. **3.** At 9:00 yesterday morning the students were studying English. **4.** In 2005 Ms. Brown was teaching in Europe. **5.** B **6.** A **7.** A **8.** A

Imperatives:
A. 1. Read the information signs. **2.** Don't touch the animals. **3.** Put papers in the garbage cans. **4.** Don't put your hands in the cages.
B. (suggested answer) **5.** Play with the elephant every day. **6.** Talk to the elephant every day. **7.** Take the elephant out for a walk every day. **8.** Sing to the elephant every day. **9.** Give the elephant a hug every day. **10.** Smile at the elephant every day.

Video Practice
A. 1 B. 1. three **2.** water **3.** move **4.** return **5.** bad **C. 1.** They live in the Arctic Ocean. **2.** They can be nine feet long. **3.** There are about one hundred narwhals in the group. **4.** They want to eat codfish. **5.** They breathe oxygen. **D. 1.** F **2.** F **3.** T **4.** F **5.** T **E. 1.** prehistoric **2.** water truck **3.** find **4.** large **5.** palaeontology team **F. 3 G. 1.** gentle **2.** worked **3.** captivity **4.** healthy **5.** animals

Exit Test
1. B **2.** D **3.** D **4.** B **5.** C **6.** D **7.** D **8.** C **9.** A **10.** C **11.** B **12.** C **13.** A **14.** A **15.** B **16.** D **17.** A **18.** D **19.** B **20.** C **21.** C **22.** A **23.** B **24.** C **25.** D **26.** C **27.** D **28.** C **29.** A **30.** A

English - Chinese Vocabulary List 中英對照生詞表
(Arranged in alphabetical order)

absolutely	當然	nod (one's) head	點頭
barbaric	殘忍	on the trail of	追蹤
bring ... back to life	拯救某生物	paint a better picture (of sth)	令人更明白
calf	幼小的牛	palaeontologist	古生物學家
close off	封鎖	pelvis	盤骨
clue	線索	promising	將來很有用
distal end	遠端	Quebec	魁北克
environmental conditions	自然環境	race against time	爭分奪秒
feel at home	放鬆	salute	敬禮
fossil	化石	shoulder girdle	肩帶
graveyard	墳場	swamp	沼澤
herd	一群	technique	技巧
husbandry	照顧動物	tide	潮汐
in captivity	被囚禁	trapped	受困，動彈不得
in time	及時	truck	貨車
ingrown feet	腳趾向內生的腳	used up	用完
jaw bone	下顎骨	vary	有差異
move around	移動	walk away from	不再這樣做